A Yoga Jungle

Brigid Mylod and Rameen Peyrow
Illustrations by Roger García

GRANVILLE ISLAND
PUBLISHING

Let's take a walk in the jungle.
We'll see trees, flowers and waterfalls.

We'll meet animals, birds and bugs.
We'll see and be the movement all around us.

. . . and powerful waterfalls
with water pouring down.

We see a round, golden moon . . .

. . . and birds
with huge wings
flying high into the clouds, then
swooping down low to the ground.

We see lizards crawling
carefully through the grass . . .

. . . and fierce cobras curving their bodies towards the sky.

We see colourful chameleons
stretching their legs . . .

. . . and great, big jungle cats arching their backs.

We see a tiny mouse curled into a little ball . . .

. . . and frogs hopping lightly onto giant lily pads.

We see jungle vines creeping towards the sun . . .

. . . and mighty gorillas with their long arms swinging from side to side.

We hear the wind blow gently through the trees
and see their leaves fall silently to the ground.

We see graceful butterflies with their wings floating slowly up and down.

We breathe like the wind,
blowing softly in and softly out.

We feel quiet and sleepy.
We lie down and pretend to be
heavy rocks sinking into the ground.

The trees and the flowers, the air and the water, the bugs, animals and people. We are all connected.

We can see and be the beauty that is all around us. Namaste.

Notes for Parents

- Practicing yoga with your child for just a few minutes each day is fun and a great way to encourage overall fitness and a healthy lifestyle.

- While reading the story and imitating the different animal postures, children will maintain and continue to develop their flexibility. They will also develop improved muscle control and coordination.

- Breathing is at the core of every yoga posture. Encourage your child to pay attention to their breath. It is their guide. If they start to hold their breath or if it becomes strained, they need to ease off the posture until their breath becomes free and easy again.

- Practice breathing with your child. You can tell them:

    Put one hand on your tummy over your belly button, the other hand on your chest. Breathe in through your nose; breathe out through your nose. As you breathe in, feel the air go into your tummy and then into your chest. As you breathe out, feel both hands sink back in. Begin with breathing in for a count of "one" and breathing out for a count of "one". Then breathe in for a count of "two" and breathe out for a count of "two". Work up to a count of "three". Try this breathing practice lying on your back and then try it sitting cross-legged on the floor with your back straight, shoulders back and chest open.

- On the following pages, the number of times to breathe in each posture is shown beside this symbol ☺. Have your child start with one breath in each posture and slowly work up to the recommended number. The most important thing for them to remember is to never hold their breath — breathing must always be free and easy, through the nose.

- While reading this book with your child, or looking at the posture description page, you can have your child try flowing through the sequence of postures moving from one to the next. At other times, your child can choose one posture and just practice that posture by itself.

- Not all exercises are suitable for everyone. Be aware of your child's physical condition and health and match the yoga postures and advice to their level and ability. Please consult a professional health care provider for more information and advice on the suitability of this exercise program before trying it with your child.

- Do not push your child beyond their abilities. Always maintain an atmosphere of enjoyment and cheerfulness. Give your child lots of praise and encouragement for trying the postures — they do not need to be perfect, they just need to remember to breathe and have fun!

Tree

😊 3

Stand with feet together. Look at a point in front of you. Lift one foot off the floor, turning knee out to the side. Slowly move foot up along leg, stopping at a point that feels balanced. Now, put palms together at chest level and slowly lift hands above head. Repeat with other leg.

Waterfall

😊 3

Stand tall with hands above head. Bend forward from waist until hands are touching the ground just in front of feet. Bend knees as much as need to, to get hands to ground.

Moon

😊 3

Stand with feet together, big toes pushing into the ground. Raise arms above head and curve them into the shape of a circle.

Bird Flying

😊 3

Stretch arms out wide, spreading fingertips. Then stand up onto tiptoes as if flying high into the air. Next, bend knees as if swooping down low to the ground.

Crane

😊 3

Crouch down and place hands on the floor in front of toes, shoulder distance apart. Then put knees onto arms as close to armpits as possible. Stay there, or try lifting toes slowly off the floor and balancing on arms.

Lizard

😊 3

Lie down on stomach, hands under shoulders, legs straight, heels back, push toes into ground. Over time, work towards lifting tummy off the floor.

Cobra

 3

Lie down on tummy, elbows bent, hands under shoulders. Push through hands to straighten arms and arch back gently, looking towards the sky. Over time, work towards getting hips slightly off the floor.

Chameleon

 3

Kneel on hands and knees, hands directly below shoulders and knees directly below hips. Keep back straight and flat, like a tabletop. Curl toes under and push backwards, raising hips towards the sky as you straighten your legs.

Jungle Cat

 3

Start in tabletop position with wrists under shoulders and knees under hips. Inhale. Exhale while pulling tummy in and arching spine towards the ceiling.

Mouse

 5

Kneel on floor, with feet together and knees hip-distance apart, hands reaching out in front, palms down. Sit back on heels. Bring head to floor as you bring hands to sides, palms facing up.

Frog

 3

Crouching down, place hands on floor in front of you, shoulder-width apart. Hop like a frog bringing legs to the outside of the arms above the elbow. Stay there. If you feel steady try lifting legs away from the floor, pushing through the hands, bending the elbows slightly.

Jungle Vines

 3

From a crouching position, reach arms alternately to ceiling as you slowly come to standing.

Gorilla

 3

Stand with feet apart, as wide as is comfortable. Turn left foot out and right foot in. Bend right knee so knee is directly over ankle. Reach arms out to the sides, shoulder height. Alternate bending right and left knee.

Leaves

 3

From standing, sway arms from side to side over your head as you slowly bend knees and come to a sitting position.

Butterfly

 3

Sit down and bend legs, letting knees fall out to the sides so bottom of feet touch one another. Slowly bring heels towards you, as close as is comfortable. Place elbows on thighs, keeping back straight.

Wind

 10

Sit in a comfortable cross-legged position. Place one hand on chest, the other on tummy. Breathe in and out through your nose. As you inhale, feel the breath in your tummy and then in your chest. As you exhale, feel both hands sink in.

Rest

 25

Lie down on your back with feet shoulder-width apart, arms alongside of body with palms facing up. Close eyes and breathe deeply in and out through the nose.